THE TURTLE
WHO WANTED TO FLY

DON OSBORNE

Dedication

This story is dedicated to my grandchildren.
Every moment I can read to you, watch your eyes light up,
and see your beautiful smiles, keeps my writing passion alive.

About the Author

Don Osborne is a first-time author of The Turtle
Who Wanted to Fly. He has been writing since a young child.
His passion for writing is poetry and children's stories.
His dream is to share with the world his love of writing.
When a child's smile lights up the room after reading
one of his stories, makes it all worth it. He has always
connected with children and, truthfully, is a big kid himself.
Having five precious grandchildren, he himself seems to always
have an audience to share his stories. He hopes all the children
who love to read, dream and imagine enjoy this book.

This story begins with a small,
brave turtle named Smalls.
His mom named him this because
he was much smaller than
his brothers and sisters.

Smalls lived in the town of Monmouth,
Maine, where he had many friends.

His best friend's name was Bare,
a tiny little black bear
living in the woods with his family.

Smalls had a wonderful imagination.
He dreamed of being able to fly one day.
Smalls loved to watch Talon, the great eagle,
soar across Cobbosseecontee Lake.

He told all the other animals about his dream
to fly and see the beauty of Maine.
Talon, the great eagle,
had told him stories of many magical places.

Sugarloaf mountain and the great Moose Head Lake.
Also, a magnificent body of water called the ocean.
He told stories of great waves and long, sandy beaches.

Smalls got so excited,
telling squirrel and bunny about these stories,
as well as his best friend, Bare.

One day, Bare got all the animals together.
He had a wonderful idea!
It just so happened it was Smalls'
7th birthday very soon.
He also included Talon, the great eagle.

He thought that maybe,
Talon could carry Smalls on
an adventure for his birthday.
Smalls was not very big,
and Talon was very strong.

Bare has seen him carrying
very large bass to feed his children.
Talon, at first, wasn't sure if this was a good idea.
He was worried that he might
drop Smalls from high above.

However, Talon wanted to make
his dream of flying come true.
Of course, they all got Smalls'
mom and dad's permission first.

It was Smalls' birthday the following day.

Bare brought him to the lake.
All the animals were gathered together there.
Smalls was surprised to see them all there.
Suddenly, they all shouted, "Happy birthday, Smalls!"

Talon stepped forward. He asked Smalls,
"How would you like to go on
an adventure and fly with me?"
Smalls was so excited
he almost jumped right out of his shell!

So it was decided. Smalls was finally
going to fly and see the beauty of Maine.

The next morning, Talon arrived at Smalls home.
Momma had some tears down her eyes.
She was a bit scared but very happy for little Smalls.

She gave him a great big hug.
Bare, his best friend, did too.
Talon grabbed a tight grip of Smalls'
shell with his claws and whisked him away.

Smalls was a bit scared at first.
Everything started to get
smaller the higher they went.

Suddenly he felt very calm and free.
The wind was blowing strong against his face.
He stuck out his four little feet and cried,
"I'm flying, Talon, I'm really flying!"

They soared for some time.
Smalls started to see roads and bridges.
Other things he has never seen before.
Talon was taking him very far,
to a place called the big ocean.
Talon told Smalls,
"They call this one Old Orchard Beach.
It is a seven-mile stretch. "

When they set down,
they landed on the warm sand.
Talon hit a bit hard.
Small's little head was peeking out of the sand.
Talon let out a chuckle. They both began to laugh.

To Smalls' amazement,
the stories were really true.
Great big waves crashing against the beach!
There were lots of big-bellied, white seagulls.
There were more humans than
Smalls had ever seen before.

Talon then showed Smalls
what humans called a lighthouse.
It is so shiny and flashing, he thought.
Talon then brought him down the shoreline.
He wanted to show him the very tall
Cape Elizabeth Lighthouse up close.

Talon explained to Smalls that
the lighthouse guides humans in
bad weather or on a foggy day.
Smalls then went into the ocean.
He said it tasted a lot different than the lake.
This water was really salty.
Talon told Smalls not to drink it.
"It will make you sick."
Talon then smiled as Smalls rode the giant waves.
He was having so much fun!

Talon let Smalls know it was time
to carry on their adventure.
He wanted to show him so much more.
They flew off high in the air.

In a flash, Talon grabbed tightly onto Smalls' shell.
Smalls wasn't paying much attention,
just enjoying the view. A sudden bang happened!
Smalls was falling down from high above.

He looked up and saw Talon locked up
with another large eagle.
Talon was in his territory, and he didn't like it.
Smalls was screaming and falling faster and faster!

He could see the ground getting closer and closer!
He quickly closed his eyes. All of a sudden,
he was gliding slowly back across the sky.
He opened his eyes and saw Talon smiling.
He was saved by his friend.

They carried on after what happened.
Talon asked Smalls if he wanted to continue.
Smalls was a bit shaken but wanted to see more.
He wasn't going to let that stop him.

Next, Talon brought Smalls to a place
called Sugarloaf mountain.
When they got closer,
Smalls' eyes became very wide.
He had never seen such a beautiful mountain.

Talon told him the elevation was 4,237 feet.
It was the second-tallest mountain in Maine.
They landed, and Smalls gasped
at how spectacular the view was.
He could see for many miles.

He had never seen so
many different trees before.
Talon spotted what Smalls only
knew as 'the great moose.'
He had heard stories but
had never actually seen one before.

It stood taller than any other animal
that Smalls had seen before.
It had an enormous,
large rack on top of his head.
Smalls looked on with such amazement.
Talon didn't appear so excited
because he had seen many before.

"Time to go now, little Smalls.
It is starting to get dark.
We need to continue our journey,"
Talon could see that Smalls was getting tired.
He spotted a cave where they
could get some much-needed rest.

The cave was a bit dark inside.
Talon could not see all the way in.
He felt it was safe for the night.
Smalls quickly fell asleep.
Talon tried to stay alert in case of any danger.

Later in the night,
Talon's eyes were getting very heavy.
He eventually fell asleep too.

Talon was awakened by Smalls' cries for help.
Smalls cried, "Talon, please save me!"

Loud growling and red eyes lit up the dark night.
Talon could see Smalls being carried away.
He knew very quickly what it was.
He was aware of the sly coyotes of Maine.

Talon spread out his massive wings
and soared quickly toward the pack.
He was focused on the one carrying Smalls away.
He lunged out his sharp claws,
piercing into the side of the coyote!

A loud cry came out of him!
The coyote suddenly dropped Smalls.
The other coyotes were close by.
Talon knew this was his best chance.

He grabbed tightly a hold
of Smalls and headed upward.
One of the coyotes lunged and
snapped viciously at Talon's wings.
He was only able to grab a
few feathers and left a small scratch.

Talon didn't care, he was only worried
about saving his friend Smalls.
Talon flew off until he spotted a large oak tree.
He glided in and landed on a large branch.
It didn't take long for Smalls to fall back to sleep.
Talon wrapped his large wings around him.
He fell asleep, too.
It had been a long day for them both.

When the morning came,
Talon and Smalls watched
the beautiful sunrise together.
High up in that oak tree,
they almost felt like they could touch it.

Talon then looked to Smalls and said,
"I have one more surprise for you."
He grabbed a hold of Smalls, and off they went.

Smalls felt like the next place
took a long time to get to.
He was eager to see where Talon was taking him.

When they got closer,
Smalls could see a lake that was massive in size.
Talon told him that this
was called Moose Head Lake.
Talon said to Smalls, "If you look closely,
you can see the outline
of a moose's head and antlers."

Smalls looked closely,
and to his surprise, he could see it!

Talon told him that this
is the largest lake in Maine.
It is 40 miles long and 22 miles wide.
It was absolutely stunning, they both thought.
Both of their eyes grew wide
when they heard growling.
Only this time, it was their stomachs.

Neither one of them had eaten
anything during the trip.
Talon let Smalls know he was
going to swoop down and get
them some brook trout.
He thought they were really tasty.

Smalls then asked if he could catch one, too.
Talon said he was willing to give it a shot.
He could easily spot those
brook trout with his binocular eyes.

They swooped down,
and Smalls missed the first time.
He felt like he had let Talon down.
Talon said to him, "Smalls,
to get better at anything, it takes practice.'

He tried several more times,
then it happened.

Smalls caught a great big one!
He had it in his mouth.
Talon was laughing so hard.
The tail was slapping Smalls in the face.
He was so proud of his catch.

They touched down on land.
They were now on one of the many islands.
That one was called Sugar Island.
They quickly did very little
talking and a whole lot of eating.

Smalls said to Talon,
"You are so right,
these brook trout are delicious!"

After they ate, Smalls said to Talon,
"Thank you for being such a great friend.
Thank you for making
my dream of flying come true."

Talon looked at him and said,
"You are welcome, little Smalls."
He then said to him,
"I think the journey is now done,
and it is time to go home now."

Smalls was ready.
He missed his mom and dad.
He also missed all of his friends.

When they arrived back home,
all the animals were around.
They couldn't wait to hear about Small's journey.
His mom, his dad, and best friend,
Bare, rushed up to him.
They gave him a great big hug and lots of kisses!
Momma asked Smalls,
"What did you see? Were you safe?"

Smalls looked over at Talon first and smiled.
Then, he said to his momma,
"Yep, we saw a lot,
and Talon kept me safe the whole time."
Talon looked over and winked at Smalls.

Smalls then thanked
all of the animals in the forest.
He told them all it was
the best birthday he could ask for.

Smalls lastly exclaimed,
"My favorite part was that I learned to fly!"

Printed in the USA
CPSIA information can be obtained
at www.ICGtesting.com
LVRC090842031023
759852LV00027B/3

* 9 7 8 1 9 1 6 7 8 7 9 7 1 *